Dear Parent:

Congratulations! Your child is taking the first steps on an exciting journey. The destination? Independent reading!

STEP INTO READING® will help your child get there. The program offers five steps to reading success. Each step includes fun stories and colorful art. There are also Step into Reading Sticker Books, Step into Reading Math Readers, Step into Reading Write-In Readers, Step into Reading Phonics Readers, and Step into Reading Phonics First Steps! Boxed Sets—a complete literacy program with something for every child.

Learning to Read, Step by Step!

Ready to Read Preschool–Kindergarten
• big type and easy words • rhyme and rhythm • picture clues
For children who know the alphabet and are eager to begin reading.

Reading with Help Preschool–Grade 1
• basic vocabulary • short sentences • simple stories
For children who recognize familiar words and sound out new words with help.

Reading on Your Own Grades 1–3
• engaging characters • easy-to-follow plots • popular topics
For children who are ready to read on their own.

Reading Paragraphs Grades 2–3
• challenging vocabulary • short paragraphs • exciting stories
For newly independent readers who read simple sentences with confidence.

Ready for Chapters Grades 2–4
• chapters • longer paragraphs • full-color art
For children who want to take the plunge into chapter books but still like colorful pictures.

STEP INTO READING® is designed to give every child a successful reading experience. The grade levels are only guides. Children can progress through the steps at their own speed, developing confidence in their reading, no matter what their grade.

Remember, a lifetime love of reading starts with a single step!

For Kelly and Kristin
—M.L.

www.stepintoreading.com
www.randomhouse.com/kids/disney

Educators and librarians, for a variety of teaching tools, visit us at
www.randomhouse.com/teachers

Library of Congress Cataloging-in-Publication Data
Lagonegro, Melissa.
  Don't be a chicken! / by Melissa Lagonegro.
    p. cm. — (Step into reading. Step 1 book)
ISBN-13: 978-0-7364-2356-4 (pbk.) — ISBN-13: 978-0-7364-8048-2 (lib. bdg.)
ISBN-10: 0-7364-2356-7 (pbk.) — ISBN-10: 0-7364-8048-X (lib. bdg.)
  I. Chicken Little (Motion picture) II. Title. III. Series.
PZ7.L14317Do 2006 [E]—dc22 2005033446

Printed in the United States of America   10 9 8 7 6 5 4 3 2 1   First Edition

STEP INTO READING, RANDOM HOUSE, and the Random House colophon are registered trademarks of Random House, Inc.

Disney's

chicken little

Don't Be a Chicken!

by Melissa Lagonegro

Random House New York

It is not easy
being a chicken.

Being a small chicken
is even harder.

Chickens are known
to get scared.

Being small can make
things even scarier.

Just ask Chicken Little.
He is picked on.

He is laughed at.

His locker is
too high to reach.

His helmet
does not fit him.

His bus driver
cannot see him.

Chicken Little does not
let that stop him.

"Don't be a chicken,"
he says.

He is brave—

even if he is small.

He warns the town
that aliens are coming!

He stands up to
big bullies.

He works hard to be on
the baseball team.

He runs miles.

He lifts weights.

He is brave
his first time at bat.

"Don't be a chicken,"
he says to himself.

He hits the winning run!
He is the team hero!

So don't be a chicken.

Be brave
like Chicken Little!

Being brave and small
can be the best of all!